# The
# LITTLEST PIG

*Written by Erica Frost*
*Illustrated by Diane Paterson*

## Troll Associates

*Library of Congress Cataloging in Publication Data*

Frost, Erica.
    The littlest pig.

    Summary: Unable to bear his brothers' and sisters'
teasing, the littlest pig in the family runs away from
home, sure that he is unloved.
    [1. Runaways—Fiction. 2. Brothers and sisters—
Fiction. 3. Pigs—Fiction]  I. Paterson, Diane,
1946-      ill.  II. Title.
PZ7.F92037Li    1986      [E]        85-14121
ISBN 0-8167-0654-9 (lib. bdg.)
ISBN 0-8167-0655-7 (pbk.)

# The
# LITTLEST PIG

There was once a piglet named
Albert. His mother was spotted.
His father was not. Albert was a
little of each.

He lived with his brothers and
sisters in a not-so-peaceful house
in the country. There were
Randy and Sandy and Candy—
and Cindy and Mindy and Max.
Albert was the youngest.

Every day they teased him.
"Hello, Half-Pint!" "Here comes
Shrimpy!" "It's Piggle-Wiggle!"
they would say.

The children slept in one big
room. At night, Mama and Papa
tucked them in and told them
not to fight. But it was always
the same: "Good night, Baby!"
"Don't fall out of the bed, Sweet
Pea!" "Aaaaal-bert! Don't forget
your teddy bear!"

One time, they made him cry.
He got out of bed and ran across
the hall. Mama and Papa made
room for him in their bed.

Mama kissed his forehead.
"They don't really mean it," she
said.
"They tease you because they
love you," said his father.
Albert thought that was a
terrible reason. And besides,
he didn't believe it, not for a
minute.

That week, he slept in his mama and papa's bed five times. He began to feel in the way.

*Maybe I should leave,* he thought. *No one will miss me. They won't even care. If they really loved me, I'd know it. There would be love signs. There would be proof.*

So that night, when everyone
was asleep, he wrote a note.
It said: IF YOU LOVE ME,
LEAVE A SIGN. YOUR SON
(AND BROTHER), ALBERT.
P.S. I AM RUNNING AWAY.

He put the note on the kitchen
table. Then he took his blanket,
his teddy bear, and eleven
cookies, and stepped into the
shadowy night.

The moon peeped through the
tree tops. The sky was filled
with stars. Far away, a train
whistled. A dog barked. An owl
fluffed its feathers and blinked
its yellow eyes.

"Whooooo?" said the owl.
"Whooooo? Whooooo?"

16

"It's only me," said Albert.
Then he hugged his bear and ate
three cookies, for courage.

He walked until he reached a
corn field. There he spread his
blanket and sat down. He was
feeling lonely, so he ate the rest
of his cookies. Then he thought
about his family.

He thought of Mama and Papa.
He thought of his sisters and
brothers. He remembered the
games they used to play, the fun
they had together. He felt a
funny feeling and wondered if
he could be missing them.

After a while, he lay down. He couldn't sleep, so he hummed a good-night song. It was the song that Mama sang when she came to tuck him in.

Sleep, my baby, sleep
   my dear,
Close your eyes and sleep.
Mama and Papa are
   standing near,
So sleep, my baby, sleep.

He hummed until his eyes
closed, and he was fast asleep.

When he woke up, he was hungry. There were no more cookies, so he picked an ear of corn. But the corn wasn't ripe and tasted bitter. He wondered what his sisters and brothers were having for breakfast.

He remembered bread and
honey. He remembered warm
milk and oatmeal. He nibbled
on the ear of corn and decided
not to think about home.

Beyond the corn field was a
small blue pond. It reminded
Albert that he was thirsty. So he
folded his blanket and continued
on his way.

A sparrow, who was mending
her nest, called to him.
"Hello, Piglet. Are you lost?
You're much too small to be out
all alone."

"I'm bigger than I look," said Albert.
He stood on his toes and puffed out his chest. But the sparrow didn't hear him. She had flown off to look for more twigs.

When he reached the pond, he
drank the cool, clear water.
Then he sat on a rock to rest.
"Ouch!" cried the rock. "How
would you like it if I sat on
you?"

Albert jumped to his feet.
"I'm sorry," he said.
But the rock hopped away.
Then Albert saw that it wasn't
a rock at all. It was a frog.
A grumpy, bumpy, brown, and
lumpy frog.

"You could have squashed me,
you know," said the frog.
"Where's your mother? Didn't
she teach you better manners?"
"She's home," said Albert.

"Home? Where's home?" asked
the frog.
Albert pointed.
"There," he said. "Past the corn
field and over the hill."

"Humph!" said the frog. "That's
a long way off. What are you
doing so far from home?"

"I ran away," said Albert. "My brothers and sisters treat me like a baby. They tease me and call me names."

"You are a baby," said the frog.
"Didn't you sit on me? Would a
grown-up pig do something like
that?"

34

"It was a mistake," said Albert.
"Anyone can make a mistake.
I said I was sorry."

"And now you want me to
forgive you, I suppose," said the
frog.
"It would be nice," said Albert.
"Harumph!" croaked the frog.
"I beg your pardon," said
Albert. "What did you say?"

"I said *Harumph!*" said the frog.
"What did *you* say?"
"I said," repeated Albert, "that
anyone can make a mistake.
Then I said I'm sorry. Then I
said it would be nice if you
would forgive me for sitting on
you."

"A very grown-up thing to say,"
said the frog. "I accept your
apology."
Then he winked at Albert, and
jumped in the pond with a
splash.
"It was nice meeting you," he
called from a lily pad. "Come
back and see me any time."

Albert waved goodbye.
Suddenly, he was feeling
better—much better. He felt so
much better, he decided it was
time to go home.

He ran past the sparrow,
through the corn field, and over
the hill. He ran and ran until,
at last, he came to his own
backyard.

There, where everyone could see, was a love sign. It was as big as a barn and painted in bright red letters. On it, were these words: WE LOVE YOU, ALBERT! PLEASE FORGIVE US AND COME HOME!

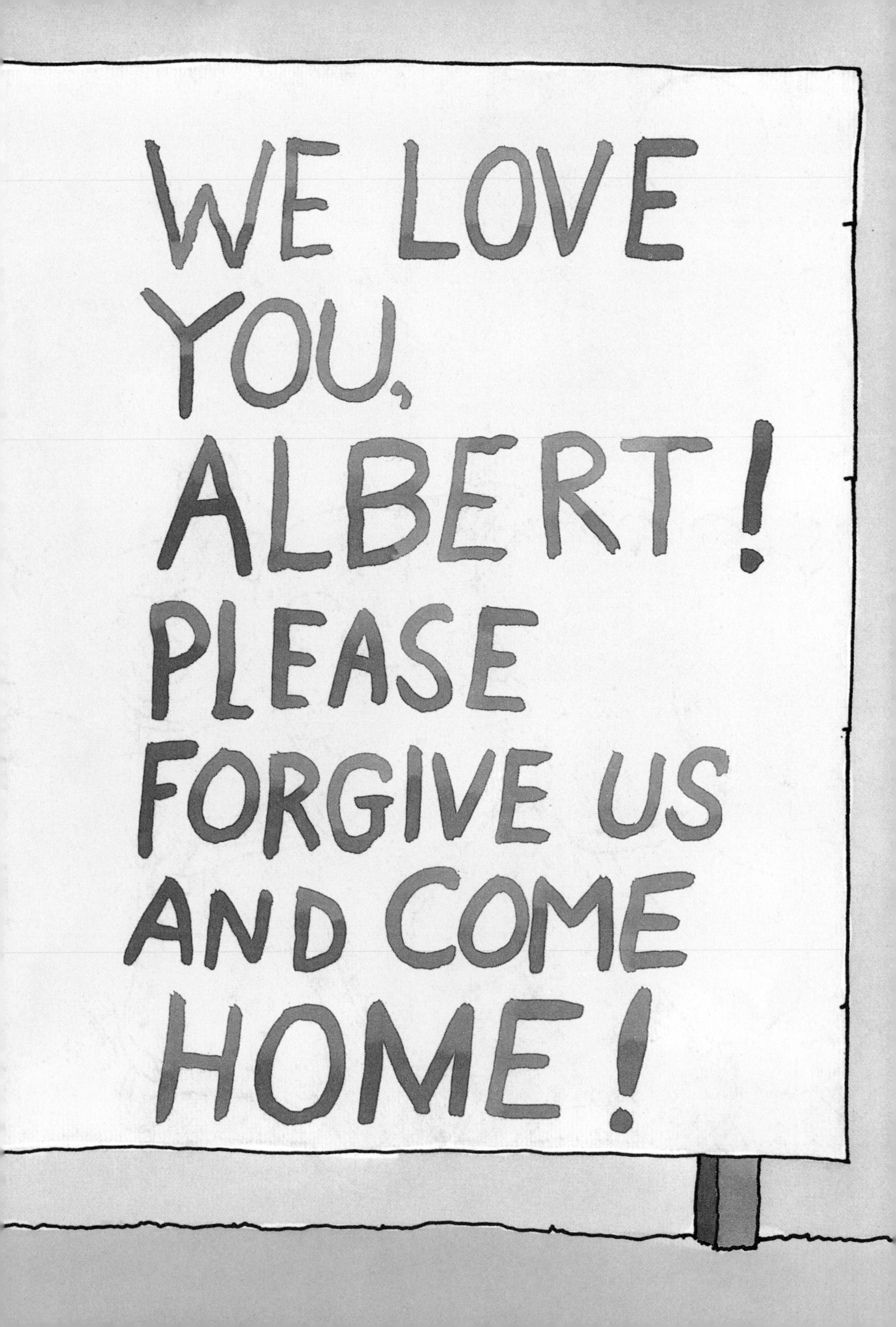
WE LOVE YOU, ALBERT! PLEASE FORGIVE US AND COME HOME!

Then, who should come running
out of the house but Randy and
Candy and Sandy and Cindy
and Mindy and Max.
"We're sorry!" they said. "We're
sorry! We didn't mean to make
you cry!"

Mama and Papa were there,
too. Everyone was hugging
everyone else—and kissing.
Then Albert said, "It's all right.
I forgive you." And the hugging
started again.

Just then, Albert remembered
bread and honey. He remembered
warm milk and oatmeal.
"I'm starving!" he said. "Let's
eat!"

And they did.